Treehouse Tales

By V. Gilbert Beers

Illustrated by Helen Endres
and Lois Axeman

MOODY PRESS • CHICAGO

What You Will Find in This Book

© 1982 by V. Gilbert Beers

Library of Congress Cataloging in Publication Data

Beers, V. Gilbert (Victor Gilbert), 1928-
  Treehouse Tales
  [The Muffin Family Picture Bible]

  SUMMARY: Contemporary tales about the Muffin family are correlated with related stories from the Bible. Includes discussion questions.

  1. Bible stories, English. [1. Bible stories] I. Endres, Helen, ill. II. Axeman, Lois, ill. III. Title. IV. Series: Beers, V. Gilbert (Victor Gilbert), 1928-   . Muffin Family Picture Bible.

BS551.2.B445   220.9.505   81-19011
ISBN: 0-8024-9571-0   AACR2

Printed in the United States of America

To Parents and Teachers

A warm summer day, a treehouse among the green leaves, and happy friends. What better setting could one find for tale-telling! Each one tells one, from Poppi to Ruff and Mommi to Tuff. There's even a tale about you! Tale-telling takes us into the imaginary world where important discoveries are made. Each Treehouse Tale correlates with an important Bible story about people of long ago. Each one brings to life some important Bible truth discovered in that story of God's people. There is a generous mixture of fun, fantasy, and timeless truths that will change lives. Your children will delight in these stories, but their lives will never be the same—they will begin to focus on Jesus.

Other volumes in the Muffin Family Picture Bible Series are *THROUGH GOLDEN WINDOWS, UNDER THE TAGALONG TREE, WITH SAILS TO THE WIND, OVER BUTTONWOOD BRIDGE, FROM CASTLES IN THE CLOUDS, WITH MAXI AND MINI IN MUFFKIN-LAND, OUT OF THE TREASURE CHEST,* and *ALONG THIMBLELANE TRAILS.*

Solomon - the King Who Had Everything

The Best Gift

1 Kings 3:2-28; 2 Chronicles 1:1-13

"When will King David choose the new king?" some of his people wondered.

David was getting old. It was time to choose one of his sons to rule when he was gone. But which one?

"Solomon will be the next king!" David said one day.

Some people were happy that Solomon was king. Others were not. They tried to hurt him. But Solomon and his friends would not let them.

Before long everyone accepted Solomon as king. Nobody would fight him anymore.

Solomon was happy that his people accepted him as king. But he wanted his people to be truly happy. He wanted the Lord to be happy with him, too.

"Come to Gibeon," Solomon told the leaders of Israel. All the leaders came. What else could they do when the king commanded them to come?

Solomon and the leaders met together at the old tabernacle at Gibeon. That was the tabernacle that Moses and his helpers had made in the wilderness many years before.

King David had moved the Ark, the most beautiful piece of golden furniture, to Jerusalem. But he had

left the big bronze altar at Gibeon.

"I will offer a thousand offerings to the Lord on this altar," said Solomon. It was hard to think of anyone offering a thousand offerings. But he did. And he did it before all the leaders of Israel. Solomon's love for the Lord was no secret.

That night the Lord talked with Solomon in a dream. "I will give you one gift," the Lord told him. "Choose what you want, and it is yours."

Solomon thought about that one gift. He wanted the best gift. But what should it be? Should he ask for gold, silver, and jewels? He could be the richest man on earth. Or should he ask to be the most famous, most important man on earth? Or should he ask to be the most powerful man of all? Or perhaps he could ask the Lord to let him live forever.

But none of those gifts seemed to be the best gift. Then Solomon knew why. They would all be for himself. The best gift must be one that he could keep on using for his people. It must be one that he could keep on using for the Lord.

"Make me a wise king," Solomon asked the Lord. "That is the best gift. Then I can serve my people better. And I can serve You better."

The Lord was pleased that Solomon asked for the best gift. "You could have asked for all those other gifts for yourself," the Lord told him. "You could have been the richest, most powerful, most important man in the world. You could have asked to live forever."

Then the Lord told Solomon about some other gifts He would give him. "You did not ask to be rich, but I will make you rich," the Lord told him. "You did not ask to be powerful, but I will make you powerful. You did not ask to be important, but I will make you important. You will be the richest, most powerful, most important man of all."

The Lord told Solomon that he would have all those things, because he had asked for the best gift. He had asked to be wise, so he could serve his people well, and so that he could serve the Lord well.

Solomon thanked the Lord and went home to Jerusalem. He was ready to serve the Lord and His people as the wisest man in the world.

Before long something happened to test how wise Solomon was. Two women had an argument. Each had a baby. One baby died during the night, and the mother put it in the other woman's arms. Then she took that woman's living baby into her arms and went to sleep.

"In the morning I found her dead baby in my arms," the second mother told Solomon.

"No, the live baby is mine," said the first woman.

"It's mine!" said the real mother.

"I tell you, it's mine!" said the other.

"Wait! Wait! Wait!" said Solomon. "I will tell you which is the real mother."

"How can he do that?" some of Solomon's officers whispered. "How can anyone be that wise?"

"Bring me a sword," said Solomon.

When someone brought a sword, Solomon gave orders. "Cut the baby in two," he said. "Give half to each woman."

"No! No!" said the real mother. "Let her have the baby. Don't hurt it."

"Cut it in two," said the lying woman. "If I can't have it, she can't, either."

"Give the baby to the woman who wants it to live," said Solomon. "A real mother would rather give her baby away than have it killed."

All the people buzzed with excitement as they left the king's palace. Before long, all Israel buzzed with excitement, too.

"King Solomon IS the wisest man on earth," they said. "The Lord has given him the best gift of all. Now he can serve the Lord and His people well."

WHAT DO YOU THINK?
What this story teaches: The best gift is one that we can keep on sharing. Solomon chose the best gift, wisdom, so he could keep on serving the Lord and His people well.

1. What did the Lord offer Solomon? What gift did Solomon choose? Why do you think he chose that gift?

2. What other gifts did the Lord give to Solomon? Why do you think the Lord gave those other gifts?

Three Wishes

Maxi's Treehouse Tale

There were once three bears who liked to sit around and talk. They talked about having a better cave to sleep in. They grumbled about the weather. And they wished that they had more honey to eat.

"Honey!" said Bo Bear. "What is sweeter than honey? I wish I had a big pot of honey to eat right now."

"Me, too!" said Jo Bear.

"And I!" said Mo Bear, who had studied his English a little more than Jo Bear.

"Ah, but all we can do is dream," said Bo Bear. "For where will we ever find a pot of honey ready for us to eat?"

"Perhaps we can help you!" a voice said.

Bo, Jo, and Mo jumped up and looked around. Who had spoken to them? Then they saw two children of the forest, dressed in green. They had little fairy wings and looked exactly like Maxi and Mini Muffin.

"Who...who are you?" asked the three bears.

"We are Maxi and Mini," one of them answered. "We are children of the forest. We have come to grant each of you one wish."

"One wish!" said Bo Bear.

"Oh, that is wonderful," said Jo Bear.

"Just what we wished for," said Mo Bear.

But the three bears stared at each other. For what should they wish?

"Honey!" said Bo Bear. "I wish I had a BIG pot of honey right here in front of me!"

Bo Bear said that so fast that he almost didn't know that he was wishing his one wish. But he was. And before he knew it, that one BIG pot of honey was sitting there in front of him.

It was the nicest pot of honey Bo Bear had ever seen. And it was all his. Bo Bear picked up his pot of honey and snogged the whole thing down without even thinking of his friends. Never once did he think of sharing the honey with them. Never once did he think of saving some for tomorrow.

Then Bo Bear propped himself against a tree. He fell fast asleep.

"He's not a bear, he's a pig!" said Jo Bear. "He could have wished for three pots of honey. Then we would each have one."

Jo Bear thought for a moment before he made his wish. Bo Bear already had his pot of honey. But he and Mo Bear did not.

"I wish for TWO pots of honey," said Jo Bear. "One for me and one for Mo."

Before he could lick his lips (or whatever bears have), two pots of honey zapped down. One was in front of Jo Bear and one in front of Mo Bear.

"Thank you!" said Mo Bear. "How thoughtful of you."

Jo Bear and Mo Bear snogged down their pots of honey. Then Jo Bear propped himself against the tree beside Bo Bear. He gave a big yawn and started to fall asleep.

"What will you wish for?" he asked Mo Bear.

Mo Bear thought and thought about that. He could wish for THREE pots of honey. That would give each of them a pot of honey for tomorrow. But what then?

"I must wish for something that will help us all," he said to himself. "But if only I could wish for something that would KEEP ON helping us all."

At last he had it! "I wish for a dozen beehives filled with bees," he said.

Mo Bear smiled (or whatever bears do when they are happy) as he propped himself against the tree. Just before he went to sleep he counted the beehives again.

"One, two, three...eleven, twelve," he counted. "Now we will have honey for all of us from now on."

But counting beehives does make one sleepy. Soon he was snoring (or whatever bears do when they sleep). He smiled as he slept, for he had learned something important–BEE careful what you ask.

LET'S TALK ABOUT THIS

What this story teaches: The best gift is one that we can keep on sharing.

1. How was Mo Bear's gift like the one the Lord gave Solomon? How was it not like Bo's and Jo's gifts?

2. Why was Bo's gift not the best gift? Why was Jo's gift not the best gift? Who were they for? How long would they last? Could they keep on sharing them?

3. What did you learn from this story? What did you learn about gifts that people give you? What did you learn about the gifts you ask the Lord to give you when you pray?

A House for You
1 Kings 5–8; 2 Chronicles 2–7

"I will build a special house," said King Solomon. "It will be a house for the Lord." It was not just any house. King Solomon and his father King David had worked for a long time to plan it.

The special house would be called the temple. It would be made from the finest wood and most precious stones.

"Will you help me?" King Solomon asked his father's friend King Hiram.

"Of course," said King Hiram. "What do you need?"

"I need your best wood and your best workmen," Solomon answered.

"And I need your wheat, wine, and olive oil," said King Hiram. "We will trade."

King Hiram's workmen went into his forests. They cut the tall cedar trees. They hauled the logs to the sea. There they tied the logs together and floated them to Solomon's land.

Before long the workmen had begun to build the special house. It would be beautiful.

"Cut the stones at the quarry," King Solomon ordered. "I do not want noise at God's house. So the men cut the stones at the quarry.

"Cut the logs far away," King Solomon ordered. "I do not want noise at God's house." So the men cut the logs far away.

The special house was put together quietly. No one pounded a hammer. No one sawed with a saw. No one shouted or made other noise. God's house was made with a whisper.

What a beautiful house that special house was! In one room golden angels stretched their wings from one wall to another. Red and blue linen covered the doorway. King Solomon put the beautiful gold chest with the Ten Commandments in that room.

The king and his helpers used the finest stones and wood for the special house. They covered the wood with pure gold. They put jewels on the walls. They carved angels on the walls. They covered the walls and doors with pure gold.

King Solomon made special furniture for God's house. He made a big altar where the priests could give offerings to God. He made a big basin where the priests could wash before making those offerings. He also made a golden lampstand that held the lamps. Those lamps gave light for the special house. The king also made a golden table. Special bread was kept on that table.

Each day the people worked on the special house. At last it was finished. King Solomon asked all the leaders of Israel to come to a service at God's house. It would be a special service, for it was a special house for God. It was also a special house for all the people of Israel.

Musicians played trumpets, cymbals, harps, and lyres. A great choir sang praises to the Lord. Then the choir and orchestra joined together in a mighty song of praise.

"The Lord is good! He will be loving and kind forever!" they sang. While that happened, the Lord came to His beautiful house in a bright cloud. That cloud shone in all of God's house.

King Solomon knelt down before all the leaders of Israel. He was not ashamed for every leader in the land to see him pray. As he knelt there he lifted his hands toward heaven and began to pray.

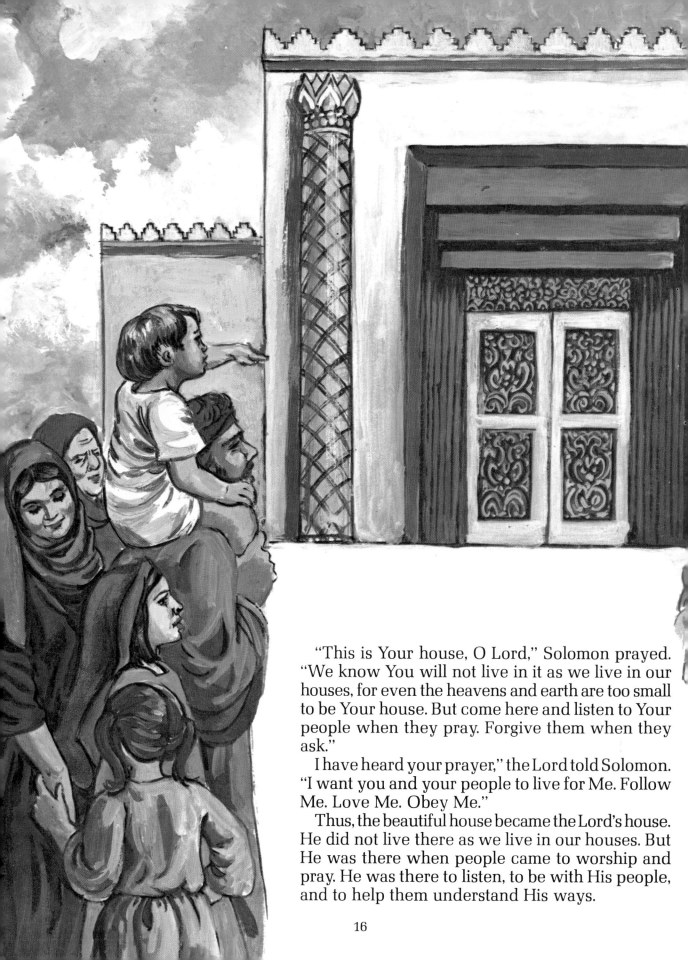

"This is Your house, O Lord," Solomon prayed. "We know You will not live in it as we live in our houses, for even the heavens and earth are too small to be Your house. But come here and listen to Your people when they pray. Forgive them when they ask."

I have heard your prayer," the Lord told Solomon. "I want you and your people to live for Me. Follow Me. Love Me. Obey Me."

Thus, the beautiful house became the Lord's house. He did not live there as we live in our houses. But He was there when people came to worship and pray. He was there to listen, to be with His people, and to help them understand His ways.

WHAT DO YOU THINK?
What this story teaches: The Lord's house was a place where His people worshiped, prayed, and asked Him to be with them. It was also a place where He listened to them, stayed with them, and helped them understand His ways.
1. Why did Solomon make a beautiful house for the Lord? Did he expect the Lord to live there as people live in their houses?
2. What would Solomon's people do at the Lord's house? What would the Lord do there?

What Is a House?

Mini's Treehouse Tale

"Why do you call this a treehouse?" Pookie asked. "It isn't a house at all."

While Maxi was thinking about that, Mini answered.

"What IS a house?" she asked.

"It's a place where people brush their teeth, eat breakfast, get dressed, and go to bed at night," he answered.

"I can show you some other houses where people don't do any of those things," said Mini.

"You can?" asked Charlie, BoBo, Tony, Maria, and the others.

"Follow me," said Mini.

First Mini stopped under the big tree by the Muffin family picnic table. "There!" she said, pointing up toward the tree.

"A birdhouse!" said Tony.

"There's one house where people don't brush their teeth, eat breakfast, get dressed, or go to bed at night," said Mini.

"Don't birds do any of those things?" asked Maria.

"They certainly don't brush their teeth," said Mini. "And they don't get dressed. But they sorta eat breakfast and go to bed at night. But I wouldn't want their breakfast or their bed, would you?"

Maria giggled when she thought of living in a birdhouse.

"How about another house where people don't brush their teeth, eat breakfast, get dressed, or go to bed at night?" said BoBo.

Mini led her friends toward her house. There was a little house by the back door. Beside it was a friendly, smiling face.

"This your house, Ruff?" Charlie asked.

"Ruff!" said Ruff.

"I have a question for you, Ruff," said Mini. "Do you brush your teeth, eat breakfast, get dressed, or go to bed at night in your house?"

"Ruff!" said Ruff.

"That means no!" said Mini. "He sorta goes to bed there, except he has no bed like our bed. Anyway, he's not a person. We're talking about houses where people don't do these things."

"What DOES Ruff do with his house?" asked Tony.

"He goes in to keep away from the rain and sun," said Mini.

"OK, how about another house where people don't brush their teeth, eat breakfast, get dressed, or go to bed at night?" said Charlie.

"Follow me," said Mini.

All the friends followed Mini down the street. At last she came to her church.

"There's another house where people don't brush their teeth, eat breakfast, get dressed, or go to bed at night," said Mini.

"But it's not a house!" Pookie argued.

"Yes, it is!" said Mini. "It's God's house!"

"Does God do those things there?" asked Tony.

"Of course not," said Mini.

"Then what does God do there?" asked BoBo.

Mini thought for a moment. She had never thought about what God does at His house. She had always thought about what she did.

"We pray and read our Bible there," said Mini.

"But what does God do there?" BoBo asked again.

"We go to Sunday school and learn about Jesus," said Mini. "And we go to church to worship God."

"But what does God do there?" BoBo kept asking.

Mini thought some more. *What DOES God do at His house?* Then she knew.

"When we pray, He listens to us," said Mini. "When we read the Bible, God's Word, He helps us know what He says. And when we worship Him,

He shows us how much He loves us. And most of all, He is there with us so that we can talk to Him and tell Him how much we love Him."

"So a house is not just a place where people brush their teeth, eat breakfast, get dressed, and go to bed at night," said Pookie.

"Not even a treehouse," said Mini.

"Then let's go back to the treehouse," said Charlie. "Because that's a wonderful place to hear Treehouse Tales."

LET'S TALK ABOUT THIS
What this story teaches: The Lord's house is a place where we worship, pray, and ask Him to be with us. It is also a place where He listens to us, helps us understand His Word, and is with us.
1. What did Pookie think a house was? What other kinds of houses did Mini show him and his friends?
2. What do we do in God's house? What does He do there?

The Richest Man of All

1 Kings 4; 9–10; 2 Chronicles 8:1–9:28

"Who is the richest man in the world?"
"King Solomon!"
"Who is the wisest man in the world?"
"King Solomon!"
That is the way people talked in King Solomon's time. There was not a wiser or richer man than King Solomon.

King Solomon was the wisest man because he had asked the Lord to make him wise. He wanted to be wise so he could rule his people well. He was the richest man because everyone gave him money and gifts.

Today people pay taxes to the government. The government is made up of many people. In Solomon's time the king was the government. He ruled the land. Everyone who helped rule worked for the king. So the people paid taxes to the king. That made King Solomon a very rich man.

Solomon's land was bigger than it had ever been. It was stronger than it had ever been. No one dared to fight King Solomon.

Since Solomon did not have to fight wars, he spent his time building beautiful buildings. He built a beautiful house for the Lord. It was called the temple. He built a beautiful house for himself. It was called the palace.

Solomon also made an ivory throne covered with gold. He made a fleet of ships and sent sailors far away to get ivory, gold, silver, apes, and peacocks.

Gold shields hung in the king's palace. Gold dishes were set upon the king's table. Gold lions stood on each side of his gold-covered throne. Gold was everywhere.

King Solomon liked horses. He liked them so much that he built cities for his horses. Those cities had

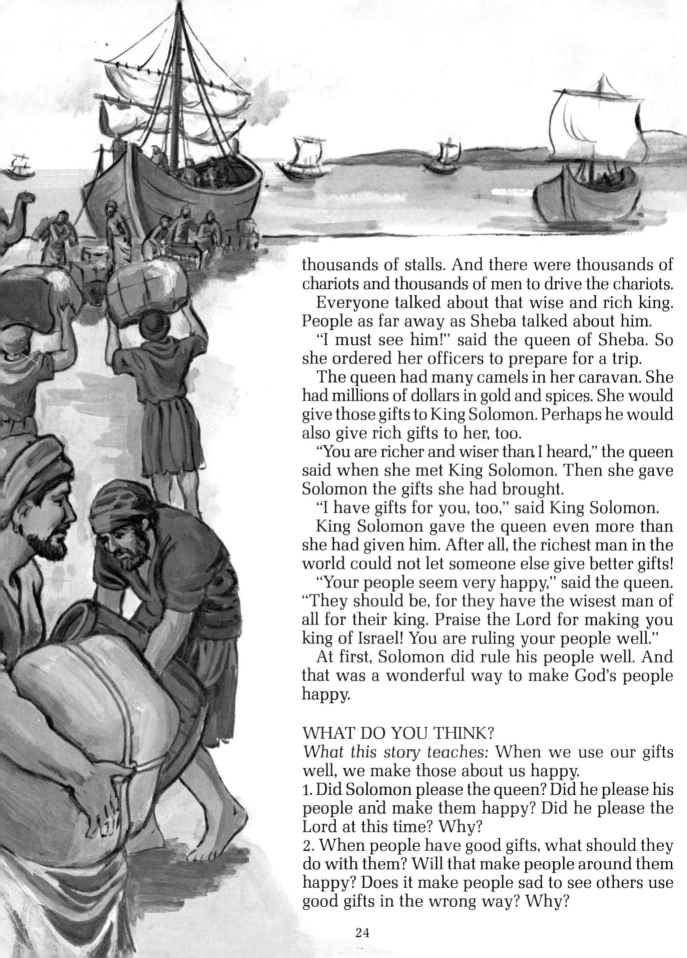

thousands of stalls. And there were thousands of chariots and thousands of men to drive the chariots.

Everyone talked about that wise and rich king. People as far away as Sheba talked about him.

"I must see him!" said the queen of Sheba. So she ordered her officers to prepare for a trip.

The queen had many camels in her caravan. She had millions of dollars in gold and spices. She would give those gifts to King Solomon. Perhaps he would also give rich gifts to her, too.

"You are richer and wiser than I heard," the queen said when she met King Solomon. Then she gave Solomon the gifts she had brought.

"I have gifts for you, too," said King Solomon.

King Solomon gave the queen even more than she had given him. After all, the richest man in the world could not let someone else give better gifts!

"Your people seem very happy," said the queen. "They should be, for they have the wisest man of all for their king. Praise the Lord for making you king of Israel! You are ruling your people well."

At first, Solomon did rule his people well. And that was a wonderful way to make God's people happy.

WHAT DO YOU THINK?
What this story teaches: When we use our gifts well, we make those about us happy.
1. Did Solomon please the queen? Did he please his people and make them happy? Did he please the Lord at this time? Why?
2. When people have good gifts, what should they do with them? Will that make people around them happy? Does it make people sad to see others use good gifts in the wrong way? Why?

King of Carrot Hill

Pookie's Treehouse Tale

"We need a king," said the folks at Carrot Hill. The "folks" were hard-working rabbits. They raised their carrots and kept their houses neat and clean. They wanted a good king who would serve his people well.

"But whom shall we choose?" some asked.

They thought of this neighbor and that neighbor. At last they chose Duke. He was a tough old fellow who had a house filled with carrots.

Duke probably had more carrots than anyone at Carrot Hill. They filled his cupboards. They were stacked to the ceiling. They were stashed under his bed. And they even poked out of the windows.

"A king must be rich," said Duke. "And I'm rich. I have more carrots than anyone else." Of course he did. Duke was so selfish that he never gave one carrot away.

Whenever a hungry neighbor came, Duke slammed the door in his face. "Those are MY carrots!" he shouted. "If I give MY carrots away, I won't be rich anymore."

Before long the people of Carrot Hill began to grumble. "This is no good," they said. "We do not want such a selfish king. We want a king who will give some carrots away." So they told Duke he could not be king of Carrot Hill any more.

"But we still need a king," said the folks at Carrot Hill. "Whom shall we choose?"

They thought of this neighbor and that neighbor. At last they chose Flip. He was a happy-go-lucky young fellow.

Sometimes Flip had a house full of carrots. Sometimes he had none. Whenever he had carrots, he had a big party. It was fun to look important. He did not give carrots to help people. He gave them to look important.

When Flip used all his carrots, he took carrots from his neighbors. "A king must have lots of folks around him all the time," said Flip. "That makes him look important."

Before long Flip had spent all of his carrots. He had spent almost all his neighbors' carrots, too.

Before long the people of Carrot Hill began to grumble. "This is no good," they said. "We do not want a king like Flip."

"But we still need a king," said the folks at Carrot Hill. "Whom shall we choose?"

They thought of this neighbor and that neighbor. At last they chose Sunny. He had lots of carrots, too.

Perhaps he had as many carrots as Duke or Flip. But he did not try to look rich. He did not try to look important.

Whenever someone was hungry, Sunny quietly shared his carrots. Whenever someone was lonely, Sunny quietly went to visit. Whenever someone needed something, Sunny did all he could to help.

"Look what a good king we have now," the people of Carrot Hill said. "He does not try to look rich. He does not try to look important. He just tries to be a good and wise king." So of course all the folks at Carrot Hill were very happy.

LET'S TALK ABOUT THIS
What this story teaches: We make others happy when we use what we have to help them, not to make ourselves look rich or important.
1. Why was Duke not a good king for Carrot Hill? Why was Flip not a good king for Carrot Hill?
2. Why were the folks at Carrot Hill happy with Sunny? What did you learn from this? What should you do with what you have?
3. Have you known folks who try to look rich or important with what they have? Do they make people happy that way? Have you known other folks who use what they have to help others? Do they make people happy that way? Which way does the Lord want us to live?

27

Time to Go Home!

Home to Jerusalem

2 Chronicles 36:22–23; Ezra 1–3

"Are you going home to Jerusalem?"

"Of course! I've been waiting for years!"

Many of the people HAD been waiting for years to go home. Long ago their fathers, grandfathers, and great-grandfathers had lived in Jerusalem. But a king had captured some of them and had brought them to a faraway land.

Now a new king ruled the land. He told the people they could go home to Jerusalem.

Some wanted to go. Others wanted to stay. They had lived in the faraway land a long time, and it seemed like home now. Their houses were there. Their work was there. Some of their friends and neighbors would stay there, too.

"Those who stay must take up a collection," the king told them. "The money will help pay for the trip for those who go." The people did as the king said.

At last fifty thousand people decided to go home to Jerusalem. They planned. They packed. They gathered in one place so they could travel together.

King Cyrus, the king there in Persia, gave them gold and silver dishes. Another king had taken them from God's house in Jerusalem many years before. Now those people would take them back. When they built God's house again, they would put those gold and silver dishes in it.

What an exciting day it was when the people were ready to go! A long caravan gathered. There were horses, mules, camels, and donkeys. There were wagons, carts, and bundles. And there were thousands of men and women, boys and girls.

A choir of two hundred men and women began to sing. They sang praises to the Lord for letting them go home to Jerusalem.

The trip to Jerusalem took many days. But as they traveled, mothers and fathers must have told their children many stories about their grandfathers and grandmothers.

There were stories about Abraham, Isaac, and Jacob. There were stories of the way Jacob's family went to live in Egypt, and how they became slaves.

30

And there was the story about the Exodus, when those people left Egypt and were free.

"Like us?" the children asked.

"Like us," said the mothers and fathers. "They went to the same land where we are going. There they made their home for hundreds of years."

"But why didn't they stay?" asked the children.

Then the mothers and fathers must have told how their people began to do things that did not please God. They turned away from Him.

"When the people turned from God, He turned from them," they said. "He let cruel kings capture them. He let those kings take them away from their land."

"And that is why we lived there?" the children must have asked.

"Yes, but now He is letting us go home," said the mothers and fathers. "He will give us another chance to live for Him. We must not turn from Him again."

At last those people came to Jerusalem. It had been the most important city in the land. Now it was nothing but piles of stones.

"We will build this city again," they said. "And we will build God's house again."

The work began. When the foundation of God's house was done, the people had a special service. Trumpets blew. Cymbals crashed. People sang and shouted for joy.

What a time of gladness that was! The people were free. They were home in Jerusalem. And they were building God's house again.

Surely now they would remember how their fathers and grandfathers turned from God. Surely they would remember not to turn from Him again.

WHAT DO YOU THINK
What this story teaches: If you turn from the Lord, you will miss the good things He has for you.
1. Why had the people been taken from Jerusalem to Persia? What had the fathers and grandfathers done?
2. Who set those people free so they could go back to Jerusalem? What did they do when they got there? What would those people remember to do?

That Girl in the Mirror

Mommi's Treehouse Tale

"Don't look at me that way!" Mini Muffin shouted.

The girl in the mirror shouted back at her.

Mini frowned.

The girl in the mirror frowned.

Mini shook a finger.

The girl in the mirror shook a finger back at her.

"Copycat!" Mini shouted. She did not like to see the girl in the mirror do everything she did.

But the girl in the mirror seemed to say "copycat" right back at Mini.

"I'm going to leave you and go away!" Mini mumbled.

Mini started to leave. But she peeked over her shoulder. The girl in the mirror started to leave, too. But she also peeked over her shoulder.

"Stop that!" Mini shouted.

"Stop WHAT?" a voice answered.

Mini stared at the girl in the mirror. Did she say THAT?

Then the voice went on. "What do you want me to stop?" Mini saw then that the voice was not from the girl in the mirror. It was from Mommi in the doorway.

"Aren't mirrors funny, Mommi?" Mini asked. "Every time I do something, that girl in the mirror does exactly the same thing."

"Don't you like that girl in the mirror?" Mommi asked.

Mini didn't know what to say. She had *pretended* not to like the girl in the mirror. But that girl in the mirror was just like her. And that girl in the mirror did EXACTLY what Mini did.

"If I don't like the girl in the mirror, does that mean I don't like me?" Mini asked.

"I have another question," said Mommi. "If you don't like what the girl in the mirror does, what can you do about it?"

Mini plopped down on her bed to think about that. Mommi went down to get dinner.

Mini was still thinking about Mommi's question when she came to dinner. Suddenly in the middle of dinner, Mini said, "I don't know."

Poppi looked up at Mini. Mommi looked up at Mini. Maxi looked up at Mini. Even Ruff and Tuff looked up at Mini.

"Now that we have your answer, what's your question?" said Poppi. So Mini told Poppi about Mommi's question.

"And I don't know," she said.

"Well, then, let's talk about it," said Poppi. "Suppose you want the girl in the mirror to smile at you. What must you do first?"

"Smile at her!" said Mini.

"What if you want her to do anything nice for you?" asked Poppi.

"Then I have to do EXACTLY the same thing first," said Mini.

"Good!" said Poppi. "But what if you happen to frown at her or stick out your tongue at her?"

"Then she will do the same thing to me," said Mini.

"That's the way it is with people," said Poppi. "God told us about it in the golden rule." Then Poppi read from Matthew 7:12.

"The Bible says to do to others what we want them to do to us."

Mini was quiet for a while. "Is God like the girl in the mirror, too?" she asked.

Now Poppi was quiet for a while. "Yes and no," he said. "God forgives us time after time. But if we turn from Him, we will miss the good things He has for us." Poppi told how the people of Israel turned away from God and wouldn't turn back. He told how God let wicked kings take the people away from their land.

"Would you excuse me, please?" Mini asked Mommi and Poppi. "I have two smiles to give away."

"TWO smiles?" asked Poppi. "Who are they for?"

"One is for the girl in the mirror," said Mini. "I want a smile back from her."

"And the other?" asked Mommi.

"The other is for God," said Mini. "I want Him to smile back at me, too."

LET'S TALK ABOUT THIS

What this story teaches: Friends have good things to share with us. If we turn from them, we will miss those good things.

1. What did the girl in the mirror do whenever Mini did something? Why?

2. Have you ever seen other people return a smile? Or a frown?

3. What did Poppi say about the golden rule? Are you keeping the golden rule with others? Are you keeping the golden rule with God?

A Time for Tears,
A Time for Joy

Nehemiah 8

"The walls are done!" the people shouted. All over Jerusalem people shouted for joy. They had worked for many months on those walls. Now at last the walls were built again.

The work had not been easy. When the people started, they worked with piles of stones. Those stones had once been part of Jerusalem's walls. But enemy kings had knocked them down. Dirt had covered them. All of those piles of stone and dirt made quite a mess.

But Nehemiah and some other leaders knew that God wanted them to build the walls again. They asked God to help, and He did. The people worked together until the walls were done.

Now it was time to celebrate! Nehemiah planned a time of joy and praise to God at one of the gates. The people came from all over the land to take part. They would praise and thank God for the work that He had helped them do. They would show Him how happy they were that they had done it.

The people became quiet as the priest Ezra stood on a wooden platform. They listened carefully as he began to read the Word of God from a scroll.

While Ezra read, some helpers went among the people. They told the people what Ezra was reading and what it meant to them.

Ezra read some, then stopped to pray and praise God. The people said, "Amen," and bowed their faces to the ground. That was their way to tell God how great He was and how they wanted to please Him.

Ezra read some more from the scroll. Again the leaders told the people what Ezra was reading and what it meant to them. That went on for hours.

Little by little the people saw what God's Word was saying to them. Little by little they saw how they had not been doing the things that pleased Him. That made them sad.

36

Suddenly someone began to cry. Then another and another and another. Before long all the people were crying. They were sad that they were not pleasing God. Ezra and Nehemiah were sad, too.

"But dry your tears," they told the people. "Today is a time for joy. We must celebrate, for God has let us build the walls. He has let us do that for Him."

The people dried their tears. Deep down they were sad and sorry for their sins. But this was a time to stop crying and rejoice. It was a time to wipe away their tears. It was a time to find what God wanted them to do. God had let them build the walls, so it was a time for joy.

The celebration went on for seven days. During those seven days the people lived in little booths. They had built the booths from branches.

During the seven days Ezra kept on reading the Word of God to the people. The people listened carefully. They tried to find what God wanted them to do. Thus, the seven days became a time of joy.

WHAT DO YOU THINK?
What this story teaches: It is a time for tears when we know that we have not pleased the Lord. It is a time for joy when we praise Him for what He has let us do for Him. It is a time for joy when we can look for ways to please Him.
1. Why did the people cry? Why did they stop crying?
2. Why were the seven days a time for joy?

Sun Smiles and Cloud Tears

Tuff's Treehouse Tale

"Everyone in the land loves Prince Maxi!" said Princess Mini.

That was true. Eveyone did love Prince Maxi. He was like the smiling sun. Some said the sun always smiled in the land because Prince Maxi smiled. So the land was always bright and beautiful. There were never dark clouds with tears.

"The smiling sun warms our land and makes it beautiful," said some.

"And the dew waters the flowers and trees," said others. "We do not need the dark clouds with tears."

As long as Prince Maxi obeyed the king's word, the sun kept smiling. As long as he did things that pleased the king, the sun kept smiling. As long as he said things that pleased the king, the sun kept smiling.

But one day Prince Maxi looked in his mirror. He thought he was much bigger than he was. He thought he was much smarter than he was. He even thought he was bigger and smarter than the king!

"I do not want to obey the king's word today!" said Prince Maxi.

So Prince Maxi told the king. He told Princess Mini. He told the people. "I will not obey the king's word today!" And he didn't!

Then dark clouds came over the land. The sun stopped smiling over that happy land. Tears began to fall. They were cold and sad tears.

The king was sad. Princess Mini was sad. And the people were sad. Even Prince Maxi was sad!

"This is no good," said Prince Maxi. "I will obey the king's word." So he did.

Then the sun smiled again. The king was happy. Princess Mini was happy. And the people were happy. Even Prince Maxi was happy!

But the next morning Prince Maxi looked in his mirror again. He thought he was much bigger than he was. He thought he was much smarter than he was. He even thought he was bigger and smarter than the king.

"I do not want to do things that please the king today!" said Prince Maxi.

So Prince Maxi told the king. He told Princess Mini. He told the people. "I will not do things that please the king today!" And he didn't!

Then dark clouds came over the land again. The sun stopped smiling over that happy land. Tears began to fall. They were cold and sad tears.

The king was sad. Princess Mini was sad. And the people were sad. Even Prince Maxi was sad!

"This is no good," said Prince Maxi. "I will do things that please the king." So he did.

Then the sun smiled again. The king was happy. Princess Mini was happy. And the people were happy. Even Prince Maxi was happy!

But the next morning Prince Maxi looked in his mirror again. He thought he was much bigger than he was. He thought he was much smarter than he was. He even thought he was bigger and smarter than the king.

"I do not want to say things that please the king today!" said Prince Maxi.

So Prince Maxi told the king. He told Princess Mini. He told the people. "I will not say things that please the king today!" And he didn't!

Then dark clouds came over the land. The sun stopped smiling over that happy land. Tears began to fall. They were cold and sad tears.

The king was sad. Princess Mini was sad. And the people were sad. Even Prince Maxi was sad!

"This is no good," said Prince Maxi. "I will say things that please the king." So he did.

Then the sun smiled again. The king was happy. Princess Mini was happy. And the people were happy. Even Prince Maxi was happy!

The next morning Prince Maxi looked in his mirror again. He almost thought he was bigger than he was. He almost thought he was smarter than he was. He almost thought he was bigger and smarter than the king. But then he saw the king behind him.

The king was much bigger than he was. The king was much smarter than he was.

Through one window he saw the bright sun, smiling over the happy land. Through another window he saw the dark clouds, waiting to bring their tears again.

"Today I WILL obey the king's word," said Prince Maxi. "Today I WILL do things that please him. And today I WILL say things that please him."

The dark clouds ran away. The sun smiled its warmest smile ever.

The king was happy. Princess Mini was happy. The people were happy. And Prince Maxi was the happiest of them all.

LET'S TALK ABOUT THIS

What this story teaches: We are happiest when we do and say things that please the Lord, and when we obey His Word. People around us are happiest when we do those things, too!

1. When did the sun shine brightest? When did the dark clouds come with their tears? How does that remind you of the people in Nehemiah's time?

2. Can you be happy when you do NOT obey God's Word? Can you be happy when you do NOT do things to please God? Can you be happy when you do NOT say things to please Him? What then should YOU do?

Brothers - Good and Bad

Two Brothers -
Cain and Abel

Genesis 4:1–16

Adam and Eve had two boys. Cain was the older brother and Abel was the younger. As they grew up, they must have played together, as all brothers do. And they must have argued and fought a little, as all brothers do.

As time passed, the two brothers grew to be men. Cain became a farmer. Abel became a shepherd, raising sheep for a living.

Cain and Abel knew that they should make offerings to the Lord. Perhaps their mother and father had told them those things. They had been told that those offerings showed one's love and honor to the Lord. And surely Adam and Eve had told their boys how the blood of a lamb was the kind of offering that would please the Lord.

Abel loved the Lord. He was glad to bring one of his best lambs for his offering. As he gave his offering to the Lord, he must have prayed and told the Lord how much he loved Him.

It seemed that Cain did not love the Lord. He did not live the way the Lord wanted him to. He would not give one of his best lambs for an offering. Instead, he put some crops he had grown on his farm on the altar.

But the Lord was not pleased with Cain's offering. He would not accept it.

Cain grew angry. He frowned and looked like a spoiled little boy.

"Why are you angry?" the Lord asked. "Why frown like that? If you obey Me and live for Me, your face will be bright and sunny. If you don't, your own sin is waiting to attack you like a fierce animal."

That was good advice. But Cain would not listen. One day he asked Abel to go with him into the fields. There he killed his brother.

Cain must have felt terrible as he saw his younger brother sink to the ground. As far as we know, Abel was the first person in the world to die. Cain and Abel had seen sheep die before, but never a person.

Cain looked for a place to hide. He wanted to hide from his father and mother, Adam and Eve. He wanted to hide from the Lord. But the Lord found him and spoke to him.

"Where is your brother Abel?" the Lord asked.

"How should I know?" Cain snapped back.

"You know!" said the Lord. "His blood is crying out to Me from the ground where you murdered him."

Cain wanted to run. But where could he hide from the Lord?

"You must go away from this place," the Lord told Cain. "Abel's blood is on this ground. You cannot farm it anymore. You cannot live here anymore. You must wander about from place to place."

"No! No!" Cain cried out. "It's too much! I can't stand it! Everyone will want to kill me!"

"But people cannot kill you," the Lord told Cain. "I will put a mark on you. No one will dare kill you with this mark on you."

Cain ran away from his farm. He ran away from his mother and father. He ran from the place where he had grown up as a boy. And he ran from the place where he had killed his younger brother.

Cain learned about a sad word called *punishment*. Ever since then others have learned about it, too!

WHAT DO YOU THINK?
What this story teaches: Doing something wrong brings punishment.
1. What does the word *punishment* mean? Can you think of some different kinds of punishment?
2. What did Cain do wrong? How did God punish him?
3. Why does God punish people who do wrong? Why do parents punish children who do wrong? Why not let those things go without punishment?

Something Worse Than a Spanking
Ruff's Treehouse Tale

"Look at that!" Maxi whispered.

Maxi looked at a hundred or more pieces of glass on the dinette floor. It had been Mommi's favorite antique plate.

Maxi looked around the dinette. Nobody had seen him knock it from its place. Nobody but Ruff.

"What will Mommi do when she knows I've broken that plate?" Maxi whispered again.

Maxi thought he would be punished. But how?

"Unless…" Maxi said to himself. "Unless she thinks someone else did it."

Maxi heard Mini's bedroom door open upstairs. Then he heard Mini coming down the stairs.

Maxi almost ran from the dinette. He quietly opened the back door and dashed outside. In about a minute he thought Mini would be in the dinette. Then he noisily opened the back door and walked in. There was Mini, looking at the broken pieces of Mommi's favorite antique plate. Maxi had timed it exactly as he had thought.

"WOW! What did YOU do?" Maxi said. He tried to look surprised.

Mini looked surprised, too. "I…I didn't do anything," she said.

Suddenly Maxi looked at Ruff. Ruff's eyes seemed to be staring at Maxi. He was SURE that Ruff was staring at him. Then Maxi looked at Mini. Her eyes seemed to be staring at Maxi, with tears in them. Maxi was SURE that Mini was staring at him.

Maxi gulped. But he had gone too far to stop now.

"Let's clean up the mess," said Maxi. "Then we'll tell Mommi that SOMEONE broke her plate."

Mommi came into the dinette while the two were sweeping up the pieces. "Oh, no!" Mommi moaned. "Not my favorite plate!" Then she began to cry.

Maxi gulped. He felt terrible now. He wanted to confess that he had broken it and that it was an accident. He wanted to tell Mini that he was sorry that he had suggested that she did it. But he had gone too far to stop now.

"SOMEONE broke your plate. We're sweeping it up," said Maxi.

Mommi looked at Maxi. Then she looked at Mini. But she said nothing. Maxi squirmed. He looked at Mini. Her eyes seemed to stare at him. He looked at Mommi. Her eyes seemed to stare at him. Then he looked at Ruff. His eyes seemed to stare at him.

But Mommi still said nothing. She quietly wiped the tears from her eyes and put the broken pieces in the garbage.

Now Maxi wished that Mommi would point a finger at him and say, "You DID do it, didn't you?" He would confess it and cry a little. Mommi would probably give him a spanking for not being honest about it. Then everything would be all right. But Mommi didn't do that. She said nothing.

Maxi ran to his bedroom. Three pairs of eyes watched him go. When Maxi looked back over his shoulder he saw three pairs of eyes staring at him. He plopped down on his bed. He felt terrible. He had broken the plate. That was an accident. Mommi probably would not have punished him for that. But he had not confessed it. She probably would punish him for that. And he had tried to make it look as if Mini had done it. Mommi certainly would punish him for that.

"But she didn't punish me," said Maxi. "She didn't spank me. She didn't scold me. Maybe I won't be punished."

Then Maxi looked up at the wall by his bed. The first thing he saw was the picture of Jesus. As he watched the picture, Maxi was sure that Jesus was staring at him, too.

Maxi didn't want to look at Jesus' picture any more. He didn't want to talk to Jesus, either. He didn't want to go downstairs. He might see Mommi or Mini or Ruff staring at him. He didn't want to talk to Mommi or Mini. He didn't want to play with Ruff. He could still see them staring at him.

"I...I guess I'll have to stay in my room the rest of my life," Maxi whispered. "I'll have to stay away from my family and Jesus forever."

Suddenly Maxi knew that he WAS being punished. This was worse than a spanking. There was nothing worse than being separated from his family and from Jesus.

Maxi ran downstairs. Mommi, Mini, and Ruff were waiting for him in the living room. He knew that they knew.

"Oh, Mommi, Mommi!" Maxi cried. "Please spank me for what I've done. Then I want a big hug from each of you. I don't want anything to separate me from my family or from Jesus."

LET'S TALK ABOUT THIS

What this story teaches: Doing wrong always brings some punishment. Some kinds are worse than a spanking.

1. What two things did Maxi do wrong? Did he deserve to be punished? What did he think when he saw Ruff, Mini, Mommi, and Jesus' picture staring at him?

2. How was Maxi punished? How was it worse than a spanking? Have you ever had a punishment worse than a spanking? What was it?

Two Brothers - Birthright for Sale

Genesis 25: 27-34

Jacob loved to hear his mother, Rebekah, tell stories. Some were about his father, Isaac. Others about his grandfather, Abraham. But the story he loved most was the one about the day he was born.

Jacob's twin brother, Esau, had been born only a moment before he was born. But Rebekah always had a twinkle in her eye when she told how the baby Jacob reached out and grabbed Esau's heel at the very time they were born.

Whenever Jacob heard that, he became quiet. He thought much about it. Esau was older. That meant he had the birthright. Boys who had the birthright got most of the family money. They even ruled the family. In Jacob's family, the boy with the birthright also received many of God's wonderful promises to the family.

Jacob wanted the birthright but didn't have it. Esau had it, but he didn't really care.

Esau often went hunting. He was a rough and tough outdoor man. So he became his father's favorite.

Jacob liked to stay home and help his mother. He liked to talk with her. So he became his mother's favorite.

One day, after Esau had been hunting all day, he came home hungry. He was so hungry that he thought he would starve.

When he came into camp, there was Jacob, cooking a pot of lentil stew for dinner. Of course Esau came to Jacob to talk about that stew.

"I'm starved!" said Esau. "How about some of that stew?"

"Of course," said Jacob. "I'll trade you some for your birthright."

Jacob must have been teasing. Who would trade his birthright for some stew? But Jacob soon learned that Esau would. Esau was willing to trade the most precious thing he had for a bowl of stew!

"I'll trade," said Esau. "My birthright isn't worth much if I starve."

"Make a vow to God," said Jacob. So Esau made a vow to God that he really was trading his birthright for the stew.

Then Esau sat down to eat and drink. Soon he was satisfied, so he got up and walked away.

Later Esau began to think about what he did. He begged Jacob to give his birthright back. He even cried. But Jacob would not do it.

It was a sad mistake. Others make the same mistake today. Those of us who are Christians are called "heirs with Christ." That means that we have a birthright. Our heavenly Father will give us the treasures of heaven.

Sometimes Christians are tempted to want some little thing more than that birthright. They are so hungry for that one thing that they forget who they are. They forget how precious their birthright is as a Christian.

Let's remember that when we are tempted to want something so much now! We must never trade our Christian birthright for one little pleasure.

WHAT DO YOU THINK?

What this story teaches: Never trade something precious for some little pleasure, even though you are hungry for it.

1. Why was Esau's birthright so important to him? Why did Jacob want it? How did Jacob get it?

2. Why is a Christian's "birthright" so important? Have you ever been tempted? Have you ever been tempted to make some little pleasure more important than your "birthright"? What should you do?

3. What kind of brothers were those two brothers? How do they compare with you and your brothers or sisters?

Hamburger, Fries, and Shake

Poppi's Treehouse Tale

"Where are you going?" asked Princess Mini.

"To the other side of the mountain," said Prince Maxi.

Prince Maxi saddled his best horse. It was a beautiful horse, almost like a friend.

Prince Maxi put a bag of gold on his horse. Then he jumped on and headed across the mountain.

But in the middle of the morning, Prince Maxi became hungry. All Maxis and Minis get hungry by the middle of the morning, even if they had breakfast.

"I'm so hungry I could eat a horse," said Prince Maxi. Of course his beautiful horse did not like that at all.

The more Prince Maxi thought about food, the hungrier he became. At last he thought he could stand it no longer.

"Oh, for a double hamburger with cheese," said the prince. "I would give anything for it."

"Anything?" asked a voice by the side of the road. "Then I will trade my double hamburger with cheese for your bag of gold."

Prince Maxi saw a little old man by the side of the road. He had the most delicious-looking double hamburger with cheese the prince had ever seen. It looked SO good. It smelled SO good.

"What good is a bag of gold if I starve?" Prince Maxi asked. He thought it sounded a little foolish when he said it. But the prince was so hungry that he traded his bag of gold for the double hamburger with cheese.

53

After Prince Maxi ate the hamburger, he knew how foolish he had been. But it was too late then.

By the time Prince Maxi reached the top of the mountain it was noon. Of course, all Maxis and Minis are hungry by noon, even if they have had a mid-morning snack.

"I'm starved!" said Prince Maxi. The more he thought about food, the hungrier he became. At last he thought he could stand it no longer.

"Oh, for a double bag of french fries," said the prince. "I would give anything for it."

"Anything?" asked a voice by the side of the road. "Then I will trade my double bag of french fries for your horse."

Prince Maxi saw a little old man by the side of the road. He had the most delicious-looking double bag of french fries the prince had ever seen. It looked SO good. It smelled SO good.

"What good is a horse if I starve?" Prince Maxi asked. He thought it sounded a little foolish when he said it. But the prince was so hungry that he traded his horse who was like a friend for the double bag of french fries.

After Prince Maxi ate the fries, he knew how foolish he had been. But it was too late then.

By the time Prince Maxi was halfway down the mountain it was the middle of the afternoon. Of course all Maxis and Minis are hungry by the middle of the afternoon, even if they had a good lunch.

"I'm starved!" said Prince Maxi. The more he thought about food, the hungrier he became. At last he thought he could stand it no longer.

"Oh, for a large chocolate shake," said the prince. "I would give anything for it."

"Anything?" asked a voice by the side of the road. "Then I will trade my large chocolate shake for your place in your family. I will be Prince Maxi Muffin, and you will stay here by the side of the road."

Prince Maxi looked at the little old man by the side of the road. He looked at his large chocolate shake. It looked SO good. It smelled SO good.

"What good is my place in my family if I starve?" the prince asked. He thought it sounded a little foolish when he said it. Then he KNEW how foolish it sounded when he said it.

Prince Maxi thought of his home and his room. He thought of Ruff and Tuff. He thought of Mini and Mommi and Poppi. He thought of all the wonderful things they did together.

"Thank you, but I will stay hungry," said the prince. "NOTHING could take me from my family, not even a large chocolate shake!"

LET'S TALK ABOUT THIS
What this story teaches: Never trade something precious for some little pleasure, even though you are hungry for it.
1. Why did Prince Maxi trade a bag of gold for a hamburger? Why did he trade his horse for fries? Why do you think he was foolish?
2. Why didn't Prince Maxi trade for the large shake? What did he learn? What did you learn?
3. How was this story like the Bible story about Jacob and Esau?

Two Brothers-Good Helpers

Exodus 4:18-31

"Lord, please send someone else!" Moses begged. Moses was talking with the Lord near Mount Sinai. He had seen a bush burning, but it never burned up. So he had gone to see what was happening.

When he did, the Lord spoke to him from the bush. He told Moses to go back to Egypt, where he had lived many years ago. He told Moses to lead the people of Israel out of their slavery and set them free.

But Moses was afraid. Many powerful people in Egypt wanted to kill him.

For many years Moses had lived in Midian. He was happy to stay and be a shepherd for the rest of his life. He did not want to go back to Egypt.

But the Lord had other plans for Moses and told him so. He must go back to Egypt to free his people.

"I...I can't," Moses argued. "I can't talk well." It must have been true or the Lord would have told Moses that it wasn't.

"I will help you talk," the Lord promised. "Since I made your mouth, can't I help you use it?"

"Please send someone else instead of me," Moses begged.

"I will not send someone else instead of you," the Lord answered. "But I will send someone with you. Your brother, Aaron, will meet you here in this wilderness. He will go with you. He will talk for you."

When the Lord stopped talking with him, Moses hurried home. He told his father-in-law, Jethro, all that had happened.

"I must go back to Egypt," Moses said. "The Lord has spoken, and I must obey."

"Go," said Jethro. "You must do what the Lord tells you."

Moses left with his wife and son. He would go to Egypt, as the Lord commanded. But first he must stop at Mount Sinai, where he had seen the burning bush. The Lord had said that his brother, Aaron, would meet him there.

When Moses reached Mount Sinai, he saw Aaron coming to meet him. "How did you know where to find me?" Moses asked, hugging his brother.

"The Lord told me to meet you here," said Aaron. "But how did you know I would be here instead of Egypt?"

"The Lord told me you would come here," said Moses.

Moses and Aaron had much to talk about. Aaron told Moses about the things that were happening in Egypt. He told how the people prayed for someone to come and set them free, for they were still slaves.

Then Moses told Aaron how the Lord had spoken to him. He told him all that the Lord had said.

"You will set our people free," Aaron said.

"And you will help me," said Moses.

The two brothers set out for Egypt. Together they would do the things the Lord had told them to do. With His help, they would set their people free. They would do it by being good helpers to each other.

WHAT DO YOU THINK?

What this story teaches: The Lord gives someone to help us when we need it. Sometimes it is our brother or sister.

1. What did the Lord want Moses to do? Why didn't Moses want to do it? What excuse did he give?

2. Who did the Lord send to Moses to help him? Do you think those two brothers were happy to work together? What makes you think so?

Two Hundred Bricks

Charlie's Treehouse Tale

"What are you doing, Charlie?" Maxi asked.

"Moving two hundred bricks."

"Why?"

"We're building a patio. The truck left them here at the sidewalk. Someone has to take them behind the house. I told my poppi I would do it for him."

"Wow! Two hundred bricks. How long will it take you?"

"TWO hours."

"Want some help? If you move one hundred bricks and I move one hundred bricks, we can do it in ONE hour."

Charlie and Maxi were ready to begin when Pookie and BoBo came along.

"What are you doing?" they asked.

"Moving two hundred bricks."

"Why?"

Then Charlie told why they were moving them. "Maxi's going to help."

"Wow! Two hundred bricks. How long will it take you?"

"If I moved two hundred bricks alone, it would take me TWO hours," said Charlie. "But Maxi will move one hundred bricks and I will move one hundred bricks. We will do it in ONE hour."

"Want some help? If you each move fifty bricks and we each move fifty bricks, we can do it in ONE-HALF hour."

So Pookie moved fifty bricks.
BoBo moved fifty bricks.
Maxi moved fifty bricks.
And Charlie moved fifty bricks.

It did not take Charlie TWO hours, as he had thought it would.

It did not take Charlie and Maxi ONE hour, as they had thought it would.

Instead, it took Charlie, Maxi, Pookie, and BoBo each ONE-HALF hour. Four friends, working together, took ONE-FOURTH as much time as one friend working alone. Four friends, working together, took ONE-HALF as much time as two friends.

When they were through, Charlie's mommi gave them a big pitcher of lemonade. "Why do you all look so happy?" she asked. "Most people don't look happy when they have been working."

BoBo looked at Pookie. Pookie looked at Maxi. Maxi looked at Charlie. Each friend really did look happy.

"It's fun to be helpers," said Maxi. "Good helpers are good givers. They're happy!"

"You're right!" said Charlie's mommi. "We were talking about this yesterday in Bible study." Then she read Acts 20:35 to them.

"The word *blessed* means the same as happy," she said. "It says we are happier when we give than when we get."

"Does that mean that the three of us are happier than Charlie?" asked Pookie.

"Not this time," said Charlie's mommi. "Maxi gave fifty bricks' worth of happiness to Charlie. Pookie gave fifty bricks' worth of happiness to Charlie. BoBo gave fifty bricks' worth of happiness to Charlie. But Charlie gave two hundred bricks' worth of happiness to his poppi."

"Then let's celebrate with two hundred bricks' worth of lemonade," said Charlie. And they did!"

LET'S TALK ABOUT THIS

What this story teaches: Someone may be there to help you when you need it. When that friend helps, it will make him or her happy.

1. Who got fifty bricks' worth of happiness by helping? Why did that bring happiness?

2. What does Acts 20: 35 say about helping or giving making us happy? Can you think of times when helping or giving made you happy? Talk about them.

When Jesus Began His Work

Preaching in the Wilderness

Matthew 3: 1-12; Mark 1: 2-8; Luke 3: 1-20

"Where are you going?"

"To hear John preach!"

It seemed that everyone was going to hear John preach. He did not preach in a church. He did not preach in a synagogue. John preached far from cities and towns. He was out in the wilderness.

"Look, there he is now!"

"And look at the crowd of people around him!"

Wherever John preached, crowds of people went to hear him. Not all those people were the kind you would expect to see there.

There were men, women, and children, of course. But there were also Roman soldiers. The people hated them. And there were tax collectors. The people hated them more. The soldiers and tax collectors worked for the Romans. The Romans were foreigners who ruled the land.

There were rich people and poor people in the crowd. And there were good people and bad people.

The people became quiet when John began to preach. He was a powerful man, dressed in rough clothing made of camel's hair. He had a wide leather belt around his waist.

"They say he eats locusts!"

"It's true! And wild honey, too!"

John's voice boomed out across the wilderness. It was almost like the voice of thunder. No wonder people became quiet.

"Turn from your sins!" John cried out. "The kingdom of heaven is here!"

John was not afraid to say what God wanted him to say. He had even told King Herod that he was

sinning. Herod did not like that. He wanted peopl to say nice things about him. But Herod knew tha John was telling the truth.

"You bunch of snakes!" John shouted. Everyon looked. John was talking to the religious leader They were standing there in their fine costume But the people knew that John was right. Those me were not living for God as they should.

"Turn from your sins!" John told the religiou leaders. It seemed strange to hear this rough ma say such things to the religious leaders.

"What about us? What should we do?" some ta collectors called out to John.

"Stop making the people pay more taxes tha they should," he answered.

"And what about us?" some Roman soldiers aske "What should we do?"

"Stop being mean to people," John answered. "Sto telling lies about others. And stop grumbling abou not making as much money as you want."

"Listen to him!" some people said. "He preache like a prophet."

"He must be Elijah," said others. "If so, he ha risen from the dead."

"Could he be the Messiah, God's Son?" other wondered.

But John was none of those. He was John, son c Zacharias and Elisabeth. He was John, cousin c Jesus of Nazareth. Some called him John th Baptizer, or John the Baptist. That is because h baptized those who turned from their sins.

God had given John an important job to do. H was to tell people to turn from their sin and tur to God. God also gave John a more important jo to do. He was to tell people that the Messiah, God' Son, had come. No wonder John preached often i the wilderness! And no wonder people came t hear him!

WHAT DO YOU THINK?

What this story teaches: We should do the wor God wants us to do. When we do, people will lister

1. What did God want John to do for Him? Di John do that? Did the people listen?

2. What was John's most important job? Who wa the Messiah, God's Son?

The Great Speech Contest

BoBo's Treehouse Tale

"Remember your birthday party?" BoBo asked Maxi.

Of course Maxi remembered his birthday party. Who could forget. Especially his last birthday party. That was the time of The Great Speech Contest.

Maxi and his friends were in the treehouse. Mini and Mommi were in the kitchen, getting the birthday cake and ice cream ready. Maria was helping.

Nobody remembers why he said it. But Pookie bragged that he would make a great speaker some day, maybe a great preacher. BoBo argued that he would be a better one. Tony modestly said that he would be the best.

Maxi said they should have a great contest to decide who was the best speaker. It would be The Great Speech Contest. Charlie would be the judge. He would say who won.

Pookie started. After he cleared his throat he began telling about his butterfly collection. He named ten different kinds before the others began to say, "BOOOO." When they booed loud enough, he sat down.

67

BoBo was next. He talked about birthday parties. He thought that the person giving the birthday party should give the gifts, except on his own birthday. He thought the idea should start now, with Maxi's birthday. Maxi shouted BOOOO so loud that all the others joined with him. BoBo grumbled that Maxi wasn't fair just because it was his birthday.

Tony gulped nervously when he began his speech. He was always nervous giving a speech, although he could "just talk" to the same people easily. "I… I'm trying to think of something to say," said Tony.

"YEAAAAH! Great speech!" said the others.

The others clapped and cheered so much that Tony smiled, bowed, and sat down. He began to wonder if he HAD made a great speech and didn't know it.

Maxi stood up, gulped, and smiled. He opened his mouth and said, "I think…" Everyone else cheered and clapped.

"Three cheers for any kid who does that!" shouted Pookie.

"Bravo! Keep thinking!" said BoBo. "Some day you may come up with a good idea."

Before Maxi could open his mouth again, Mini opened the kitchen door. "CAKE AND ICE CREAM IS ON! COME AND GET IT!" she shouted.

The Great Speech Contest was suddenly over. There was a wild scramble for the kitchen door.

About halfway through the cake and ice cream, Charlie stood up. "I have a winner!" he said.

"Bravo!" shouted Tony. "Charlie's cake has won a beauty contest."

"Wise guy!" Charlie mumbled.

"A winner of what?" asked BoBo. "Are we having a see-who-can-eat-cake-and-ice-cream-the-fastest contest?"

"Have you guys forgotten that we never finished our Great Speech Contest?" asked Charlie. "Remember? I'm the judge."

"Yeah! That's right! Did I win, Charlie?" asked Tony.

"If you will all be quiet, I'll declare the winner," said Charlie. So everyone became quiet.

"The winner of The Great Speech Contest is... MINI MUFFIN!" Charlie proclaimed.

"Mini?" asked Tony. "But she didn't give a speech."

"Oh, yes she did!" said Charlie. "You guys mumbled about things that weren't important. Mini spoke, and it was important. In fact, it was so important that five big guys dropped everything and ran to do what she said."

Mini blushed. "But what was my speech, Charlie?"

"CAKE AND ICE CREAM IS ON! COME AND GET IT!" Charlie repeated. "That was important information. It was right to the point. It told us what to do. Then every one of us ran to do it. A great speech!"

Mini bowed. "But what did I win?" she asked.

"Thirds on cake and ice cream!" said Charlie. So Mini had thirds while all the others had seconds. The Great Speech Contest ended with one embarrassed little "urp."

LET'S TALK ABOUT THIS

What this story teaches: People will listen when we have something important to say.

1. Why didn't the others listen to Pookie's speech? What about BoBo's, Tony's, and Maxi's? Why did everyone listen to Mini's speech? What did they do about it?

2. John the Baptist had something important to say. What was it? Why did people want to DO something when he spoke?

3. Have you said something important about Jesus lately? Start by telling friends that He is your best friend. Ask if they would like Him to be their best friend, too. He will be if they ask Him to be.

When Jesus Was Baptized

Matthew 3: 13-17; Mark 1: 9-11; Luke 3: 21-22

"Is he the Messiah?" people whispered.

"Let's ask him!" said some.

John preached like a prophet. He was brave, not afraid to tell people about their sins. He did not live like a rich man in the city. Instead, he lived like a poor man in the wilderness where he preached.

Some people thought he was the prophet Elijah who had come back to life. Others thought he was the Messiah, God's Son, who was coming some day.

So some people asked John who he was.

"Are you Elijah, come back to life?" some asked.

"No, of course not!" John answered.

"Are you the Messiah, God's Son?" others asked.

"No! He is coming soon. But He is much greater than I am. I am not even good enough to untie His sandals," John answered.

"Who IS this much greater Person?" the people wondered.

One day John was baptizing people in the Jordan River, as he often did. Suddenly a Man stepped out

from the crowd. He waded into the Jordan River to the place where John stood. Then He asked John to baptize Him.

John looked up into the Man's face. It was his cousin Jesus, from Galilee. But John knew that He was more than his cousin. John knew that He was the Messiah, God's Son.

"No, You must not ask me to baptize You," John told Jesus. John had already said he was not good enough to untie His sandals. "You should baptize me instead!"

"But you must baptize Me," Jesus told John. "That is part of God's plan." Jesus was not like the others. He did not need to turn from sin, for He had never sinned.

But Jesus must be an example to everyone else. How could God ask others to be baptized unless Jesus was baptized?

At last John knew what Jesus meant. Jesus must be baptized. And Jesus was asking him to do it.

So John baptized Jesus in the Jordan River. When Jesus came up out of the water something wonderful happened. The heavens opened, and the Spirit of God came down like a dove. Then the Spirit of God, like a dove, flew down upon Jesus.

A voice called from heaven. It was the voice of God.

"This is My Son. I love Him. And I am pleased with Him," the voice of God said.

Who heard the voice? Who saw the dove? The Bible does not say. It does not tell us if the people in the crowd saw and heard. But certainly John and Jesus saw and heard. And perhaps some who became Jesus' apostles were in the crowd that day and they, too, saw and heard.

Matthew, Mark, and Luke wrote the story in their books, now in our Bible. Now we know about the day when God spoke from heaven. Now we know that God Himself said that Jesus is His Son. We can be thankful that Matthew, Mark, and Luke have told us, too.

WHAT DO YOU THINK?
What this story teaches: Jesus did things that were part of God's plan.
1. Why did many people ask John to baptize them? What did that show?
2. But Jesus had never sinned. So His baptism did not show that He was turning from sin. What did it show?

The Poppi Barometer

Maria's Treehouse Tale

"Why did he say partly cloudy?" Maria asked.

Maria's poppi smiled. "What should he say?" he asked.

"Partly sunny!" said Maria. "Partly cloudy sounds gloomy. Partly sunny sounds happy."

"Very good!" said Maria's poppi. "We should have you write the weather forecasts."

"Clouds are like frowns," said Maria. "Suns are like smiles."

"When I smile, is my weather sunny?" asked Maria's poppi. "And when I frown, is my weather cloudy?"

"Oh, Poppi!" said Maria. "That gives me a wonderful idea. I'll make a Poppi Barometer. When I do something that pleases you, I'll put a little sun on it. When I do something that doesn't please you, I'll put a little cloud on it."

"That is a wonderful idea, Maria," said her poppi. "But I have another idea. It will help you to CHANGE

73

the weather on the Poppi Barometer before it happens."

Maria's eyes opened wide. "How?" she asked.

"Suppose you are about to do something that will NOT please your poppi. What will you see yourself doing later?"

"Putting up a little cloud."

"But you haven't put up the cloud yet, have you?"

"No."

"And if you do something that WILL please your poppi instead, will you put up the cloud?"

"No, Poppi! I will put up a sun instead of the cloud."

"So whenever you are getting ready to do something, you can ask if it will bring a cloud or sun on the Poppi Barometer. Right?"

"Right!"

"And before you do it, you can change it from something that will bring a cloud to something that will bring a sun."

"That is a wonderful idea, Poppi!"

"Maria, have you thought of a Jesus Barometer?"

"A Jesus Barometer? Oh, Poppi! That is another wonderful idea. When I do something to please Him, I will put up a sun. When I do something that doesn't please Him, I'll put up a cloud."

"Good, Maria. And when you are getting ready to do something that will cause a cloud on the Jesus Barometer, you can change that to something that will bring on a sun."

"Oh, Poppi. I don't want to put a cloud on my Jesus Barometer. The next time I do something, I'll make sure it will bring a sun."

"Good, Maria. Now I'll help you make those two barometers."

"But, Poppi! Do we need two? If I please Jesus, you will be pleased. If I do something that doesn't please Jesus, you won't be pleased, either."

"That's right, Maria. Let's make one – the Jesus Barometer. Whatever you do to please Jesus will please me, too."

LET'S TALK ABOUT THIS

What this story teaches: We should each want to please our parents. And we should each want to please Jesus. Jesus pleased His Father in heaven.

1. Do you remember why Jesus was baptized? What did He say about wanting to please His Father in heaven?

2. Do you like to please your father or mother? Why?

3. Do you like to please Jesus? Remember Maria's suns and clouds when you are about to do something. Will it please Jesus? Do it. Will it not please Him? Then do something else that will please Him.

When Jesus Was Tempted

Matthew 4: 1-11; Mark 1: 12-13; Luke 4: 1-13

John watched quietly as Jesus walked from the Jordan River. God's voice was still ringing in his ears. "This is My Son. I love Him. And I am pleased with Him." There was no question about Jesus now. John knew for sure that Jesus was God's Son. God had said so Himself.

John must have wondered what Jesus would do now. Where would He go?

Jesus made His way through the crowd. Then He walked alone through the wilderness west of the Jordan River. He climbed up into the lonely hills at the edge of the wilderness. No one else would be up there. Jesus could be alone to talk with His Father in heaven.

During the next forty days and nights Jesus ate no food. He thought and He prayed. He talked often with His Father about the work ahead. Perhaps they talked about the twelve men whom Jesus would choose to be His disciples. Perhaps they talked about the miracles that Jesus would do and the sermons He would preach. And perhaps they talked about the day Jesus would die on the cross.

Then one day the devil came to see Jesus. Jesus was not surprised. He knew that would happen. The

devil would try to stop Him. He would tempt Jesus to give up the work God wanted Him to do.

"If You are God's Son, make these stones become bread," the devil told Jesus. Jesus was hungry. He had not eaten for forty days. Would it be wrong to turn one of those round stones into a loaf of bread? He could do it easily. But Jesus knew He must not do it. That would please the devil. It would not please God.

"Bread is not the only food," Jesus told the devil. "The Word of God is more important than bread."

The devil knew that he had lost that time. But he would try again.

So the devil took Jesus into Jerusalem. They went to the highest point on the wall around the temple. It was called the pinnacle.

"If You are God's Son, jump down," the devil said. "Angels will come and save You–if You really are God's Son." Would it be wrong to jump? That would show the devil that He really was God's Son. But it would also please the devil, for Jesus would do what the devil said. No, He must not do it.

"The Word of God says you must not tempt the Lord your God!" Jesus answered. He was telling the devil, "Since I AM God's Son, you must not tempt Me."

The devil knew that he had lost again. He would try once more. This time he took Jesus to the top of a high mountain. He showed Jesus all the kingdoms of the world. He showed Jesus how much power and glory he had in those kingdoms.

"I will give You all of these if You will bow down and worship me," the devil told Him. But Jesus knew that He must choose God or the devil. He could not worship both.

"Go away!" Jesus told the devil. "The Word of God says you must worship the Lord your God only. You must serve Him alone."

The devil had lost the third and last time. He had tried three times to tempt Jesus. But each time Jesus won. Each time Jesus told what the Word of God said. So the devil went away. Then angels came and took care of Jesus.

WHAT DO YOU THINK?
What this story teaches: Jesus was tempted, but He won by telling what the Word of God said.
1. What did the devil try to get Jesus to do? Why would Jesus want to do each of those three things?
2. What did Jesus tell the devil each time? Why do you think Jesus won each time?

Sir Anthony and the Dragon

Tony's Treehouse Tale

"Sir Anthony, please rise and come forward!"

Tony (that is, Sir Anthony) quickly stepped up to the throne where Prince Maxi was sitting. He bowed with one knee to the floor.

"There is a terrible dragon in our kingdom, Sir Anthony," said Prince Maxi. "His name is TEMPTATION. Find him, and chase him from our kingdom."

Sir Anthony bowed again.

"Use any sword you choose in the royal sword room," said Prince Maxi. "If you chase him away, you will be known as Sir Anthony the Dragon Chaser."

Sir Anthony bowed twice that time. Then he went to the royal sword room. He saw three swords hanging on the wall. One was named STRENGTH.

"That's the one!" said Sir Anthony. "If I am strong, I will chase the dragon TEMPTATION from our kingdom." So he took the sword named STRENGTH and went out to find the dragon.

No one has to look for TEMPTATION very long. Before he could say "dragon" Sir Anthony found him. Or did the dragon TEMPTATION find Sir Anthony?

Sir Anthony lifted his sword, STRENGTH. But before he could do anything, the dragon blew a blast from his nostrils. Sir Anthony fell to the ground, coughing and sneezing. TEMPTATION chuckled a funny dragon chuckle.

"This sword won't do!" said Sir Anthony. "Back to the royal sword room!"

In the royal sword room Sir Anthony looked at the other two swords on the wall. One was named WISDOM.

"That's the one!" said Sir Anthony. "If I am wise, I will chase the dragon TEMPTATION from our kingdom." So he took the sword named WISDOM and went out to find the dragon.

No one has to look for TEMPTATION very long. Before he could say "dragon" Sir Anthony found him. Or did the dragon TEMPTATION find Sir Anthony?

Sir Anthony lifted his sword, WISDOM. But before he could do anything, the dragon blew a blast from his nostrils. Sir Anthony fell to the ground, coughing and sneezing. TEMPTATION chuckled a funny dragon chuckle.

"This sword won't do!" said Sir Anthony. "Back to the royal sword room!"

In the royal sword room Sir Anthony looked at the last sword on the wall. It didn't look as much like a sword as the other two. But somehow he felt that must be the right one. That sword was named THE WORD. So Sir Anthony took the sword named THE WORD and went out to find the dragon.

No one has to look for TEMPTATION very long. Before he could say "dragon" Sir Anthony found him. Or did the dragon TEMPTATION find Sir Anthony?

Sir Anthony lifted his sword named THE WORD. The dragon TEMPTATION did not chuckle when he saw that. He took one look at it and turned from it and ran as fast as he could run.

"Sir Anthony the Dragon Chaser!" Prince Maxi said later as Sir Anthony bowed before him. "I now give that honor to you."

"Thank you, Prince Maxi," said Sir Anthony. "But the honor does not belong to me. It belongs to this wonderful sword."

LET'S TALK ABOUT THIS

What this story teaches: When you are tempted, use the Word of God to chase it away.

1. Why didn't Sir Anthony's first sword chase the dragon TEMPTATION away? Why didn't his second sword do it?

2. Why did the third sword do it? What was the third sword? How does this remind you of the Bible story of Jesus' temptation? What will you do the next time you are tempted? What will you fight with?

Working Together - Working Against

Working Together against God - Ananias and Sapphira

Acts 5: 1-11

People all over Jerusalem were talking about Jesus. As soon as He went back to heaven, His friends told their friends. Then those friends told other friends. Before long it seemed that everyone in Jerusalem was talking about Jesus.

Many accepted Jesus as their Savior. Before long there were about five thousand who believed in Him.

The "believers," as they were called, lived differently from other people in Jerusalem. They loved each other. They helped each other. They even sold their things to share with each other.

Before long there were many believers who sold their things to help other believers. Peter set up

a table. People brought their money to him. Then he shared it with believers who needed it most.

Joseph of Cyprus sold what he had and gave the money to Peter. But there was something special about the way he did it. He gave his money in such a loving way that people said, "What an encouragement he is." They even nicknamed him Barnabas. That meant "son of encouragement."

Ananias and his wife, Sapphira, heard what Barnabas had done. They heard how all the believers said good things about Barnabas. They wanted those people to say good things about them, too. But they didn't want to give up all their money, as Barnabas had done.

Then Ananias had a plan. "We will sell our land, just as Barnabas did," he told Sapphira. "We will tell Peter that we are giving ALL our money. But we will keep most of it for ourselves. Then we can have our money and have the people say good things about us, too!"

Sapphira thought that was a wonderful idea. She wanted to work with Ananias to make it happen.

As soon as they sold the land, Ananias counted part of the money. He put it in a bag and took it to Peter.

"Sapphira and I have sold our land," he said. "We want to give ALL the money."

But Peter knew. The Lord had already told him

about Ananias and Sapphira. He had told Peter how they were working together AGAINST Him.

"Ananias, why are you doing this?" Peter asked. "Satan is causing you to lie to the Lord! The land was yours, to keep or sell. When you sold it, the money was yours, to keep or give away. So why pretend to give all when you know you are lying? But you are lying to God, not to men."

Ananias was afraid when he heard what Peter said. Nobody was saying good things about him and Sapphira now! Peter knew that he and Sapphira were working together against God. Now everyone else knew it, too.

Ananias was so afraid that he died and fell to the floor. Some young men with Peter wrapped his body in strips of cloth, as they did in those days. Then they buried him.

About three hours later Sapphira walked in. She wanted to hear all the good things people were saying about her and Ananias. She had not heard yet what had happened.

"Did you sell your land for this amount?" Peter asked Sapphira.

"Yes, exactly!" she answered.

"Then you two have worked together to lie to God," Peter said. "The young men who buried Ananias will now bury you."

Sapphira died and fell to the floor, just as Ananias had done. Then the young men buried her with Ananias.

The other believers were afraid when they heard that. But they knew now how terrible it is to work together against God.

WHAT DO YOU THINK?
What this story teaches: Ananias and Sapphira were bad examples of working together for God. They showed us how terrible it is to work together against Him.
1. What did Ananias and Sapphira do? How were they working together?
2. Did that please God? Why not? Can you think of some ways you and your friends have ever worked together against God? What did you learn from this story?

The Winner!
Big Bill's Treehouse Story

"That's not fair!" Pookie complained. "You've got Big Bill Bluffalo on your side."

"We've also got Mini!" Maxi argued. "So the three of us should equal the three of you."

"He's right!" BoBo added, siding with Maxi. "If Pookie, Charlie, and I can't outpull those three, we're cream puffs."

Somehow, someone had started the idea of a rope pulling contest. Maxi, Mini, and Big Bill against Pookie, Charlie, and BoBo. Mini couldn't do much, but Big Bill would make up for her.

Charlie hauled some rope from his garage. Tony said he would be the referee. Maria decided she would make a good cheerleader.

"OK, keep it clean!" Tony said, trying to sound important.

Charlie, Pookie, and BoBo got on one end of the rope. Maxi, Mini, and Big Bill got on the other end. They really did make a strange-looking team!

"Ready?" asked Tony.

"Ready on this end," said Charlie.

"Ready on this end, too," said Maxi.

"Then PULL!" shouted Tony.

Maxi, Mini, and Big Bill pulled as hard as they could. Charlie, Pookie, and BoBo pulled as hard as they could. But neither side could pull the other over the line.

"Pull harder!" Maxi shouted at Big Bill.

"I am!" Big Bill grumbled.

"Go team, go!" shouted Maria. She tried to cheer equally for each side. That way, she was sure to be cheering for the winning team.

But still both teams were equal. Neither could pull the other across the line.

"PULL HARDER, you big buffalo!" Maxi shouted at Big Bill.

There are some things you shouldn't say, even when you think them. That was one!

"OK, you little shrimp, I WILL!" Big Bill shouted.

As soon as he said that, Big Bill left Maxi's and Mini's side of the rope. He went over to Charlie's and Pookie's and BoBo's side of the rope.

With one mighty UNGHHH, Big Bill, Charlie, Pookie, and BoBo pulled Maxi and Mini into a pile of squirming rope pullers.

"We won!" shouted Pookie.

"Yeah, we're the greatest rope pullers," added BoBo.

Maxi and Mini wanted to say a few things. But when it's four against two, some things are better not said. Especially when one of the four is Big Bill.

The big rope pulling contest was over. Maxi and Mini headed home.

That night after dinner, Maxi was still brooding about the way things went. He almost didn't hear what Poppi said when he read the Bible story. It was about Ananias and Sapphira. Then Poppi asked if anything exciting had happened that day. Maxi told about the rope pulling contest and what Big Bill had done.

Poppi thought for a moment. "Ananias and Sapphira were like that," he said at last.

Maxi and Mini looked puzzled. "How?" Maxi asked.

"Everyone thought that Ananias and Sapphira were pulling on God's end of the rope, pulling with Him," said Poppi. "Suddenly the two of them went to the other end. Both started pulling the other way. Before long, things wound up in a big pile."

Poppi looked at Maxi and Mini. "You learned something more important than winning a rope pulling contest," he said. "We must each pull FOR someone or AGAINST someone. We must either pull FOR God or AGAINST God."

"I want to pull FOR God," said Maxi.

"Me, too!" said Mini.

"Then the rope pulling contest made you a REAL winner!" said Poppi. "A real winner on God's side."

LET'S TALK ABOUT THIS
What this story teaches: Working together against God is sad to see. If you are not working FOR Him, you are working AGAINST Him.
1. What happened when Big Bill went from one team to the other? How did Poppi compare that to Ananias and Sapphira?
2. Read Luke 11: 23. What did Jesus say? How can you pull FOR Jesus? How can you pull AGAINST Jesus? Which do you want to do?

Working Together for God - Aquila and Priscilla

Acts 18: 1-11, 18-19, 24-26

"I have good news for you!" Paul said wherever he went. He told people about Jesus. He went to this city. He went to that city. He told how Jesus had died for them.

Some people believed. Others did not. Some even laughed at Paul and his good news.

But Paul kept on going from city to city. He kept on telling people the good news.

One day Paul went to Greece. He went to a big city there called Athens. He had never been there before.

"What will the people think?" he wondered. "What will they do?"

Paul climbed to the top of a hill. He told the people there about Jesus. But the people would not believe.

"I will go to another city here in Greece," said Paul. He went to a city called Corinth.

"What will these people think?" he wondered. "What will they do?"

Paul told the people there about Jesus. Most of them would not believe. Only a few did.

Paul needed a friend. Then he met a man named Aquila and his wife Priscilla. They made tents to sell. So did Paul. They had been chased out of a city because of what they believed. So had Paul.

"Stay at our house, and make tents with us," they told Paul. So he did. Before long Paul and they were good friends.

While they made tents together, Paul told Priscilla and Aquila about Jesus. They listened. Then they accepted Jesus as their Savior. They began to help Paul tell others about Jesus.

Each day Paul went to a room to tell others about Jesus. Some believed. Others did not. Some people

would have quit. Perhaps Paul wanted to, too.

"You must not quit!" the Lord told Paul one night. "Keep on telling people about Jesus. I will be with you."

Paul kept on telling the people at Corinth about Jesus. Before long there was a little church. Priscilla and Aquila worked with Paul in this church.

At last it was time for Paul to leave Corinth. "We will go with you," said Priscilla and Aquila. They wanted to work together for God in other places.

So the three sailed off to a place called Ephesus. Paul had to go on. But Priscilla and Aquila stayed there and worked together with the people who had believed in Jesus.

One day a man named Apollos came to town. He spoke to the people. He was a wonderful speaker. He talked about God. But he did not know about Jesus. So Priscilla and Aquila told Apollos about Him. They asked him to come to their house for dinner. They helped Apollos accept Jesus as his Savior.

Apollos spoke again. That time he spoke about Jesus. Then he worked with Priscilla and Aquila. The three of them worked together for Jesus.

That's the kind of working together that pleases Jesus, isn't it?

WHAT DO YOU THINK?

What this story teaches: Priscilla and Aquila were good examples of working together for God. They showed us how good it is to work together for Him.

1. Do you remember the story of Ananias and Sapphira? What did they do together? Did that please Jesus? Why not?

2. What did Priscilla and Aquila do together? Did that please Jesus? Why?

3. How can you work together with others for Jesus?

A Story about YOU

Your Treehouse Tale

This is YOUR treehouse tale. Your name may be Mary or John or Joe or Kathy. But whatever it is, whenever you see ☺, say YOUR name. If there are two or more of you reading this, say them all whenever you see ☺. This is the tale about the day, today, when you go to play with Maxi and Mini at their house. Ready?

"Mommi! Poppi! Guess who's coming to play with us today?" Mini and Maxi shouted.

"Who?" asked Poppi.

"☺!" said Maxi *(don't forget to say YOUR name)*.

"Oh, dear," said Mommi. "I hope the house is clean. What if ☺'s mommi comes, too?"

"Don't worry about that," said Poppi. "☺'s mommi understands those things. She would probably be worried if you dropped in with Maxi or Mini."

Mommi laughed. "She shouldn't be," she said, "I'm just plain Mommi Muffin."

"Good! Now we've settled that," said Poppi. "So let's all pitch in and help plain Mommi Muffin clean up the place. She will feel better if the house is clean and neat when ☺ comes."

Mommi ran the vacuum. Mini dusted. Maxi straightened the furniture. Poppi shook out the carpets. Before long the house was neat and clean.

"See what happens when we work together?" said Poppi. "Mommi and I have always worked together. And we always get things done. Besides, we always have fun doing it together."

"I was just thinking," said Mini.

"Trying something new, Mini?" asked Maxi.

"But I was thinking how nice it would be if ☺ could have seen how we work together," said Mini. "Now all ☺ will see is a nice neat house, and not how the Muffin family does things together."

"I guess you will have to tell ☺ how we do things together," said Poppi. "But don't forget to tell WHY we do things together. What will you tell ☺?"

"Because we love each other," said Mini.

"And families who do good things together have fun together," said Maxi.

"There's something else you should tell ☺," said Poppi. "People in God's family should do

things together, too. They should be like our family, doing things together because they love each other."

While Maxi and Mini waited for ☺ to come, Poppi read the Bible story about Priscilla and Aquila. "See how much they did for God by working together?" Poppi asked.

"We'll be glad when ☺ comes," said Mini. "Then we can do things together, too."

Maxi and Mini almost jumped when the doorbell rang. "It's ☺!" said Maxi.

Then Maxi and Mini ran to the door and opened it.

And there you were! (Hope you have fun TOGETHER today with Maxi and Mini.)

LET'S TALK ABOUT THIS
What this story teaches: It is good to do things together. It is also fun. It is especially good to do things together for God.

1. How did you like being part of this story? Would you like to do things together with Maxi and Mini some afternoon?

2. Do you like to do things together with your family? Do you like to do things with others? Think of some things you can do with others for Jesus. Then talk about how you can do them.

Mini's Word List

Twelve words that all Minis and Maxis want to know:

BAPTIZE – Jesus was baptized in the Jordan River. John the Baptist did that with the water of the river. Some Christians believe John put Jesus under the water for a moment. Others believe John poured water on Jesus. Still others believe John sprinkled water on Jesus. People today are baptized in one of those three ways. Putting people under the water and lifting them out is called *immersion*. It shows how people are buried with Jesus and raised up to new life.

PALACE – The house where a king lived. A palace was usually much nicer than other houses.

PRAISE – We praise someone when we say good things about them. We praise God when we tell Him or others how wonderful He is.

PUNISHMENT – When we do things wrong we are usually punished for them. Punishment hurts. Because it hurts, we try not to do wrong things so we won't be punished.

QUARRY – A place where stone is cut and taken from the earth. Solomon's workers got the stone for the temple from a quarry.

SCROLL – Some books in Bible times were scrolls. They were long sheets rolled on two rollers. The sheets were usually made from the stems of plants called papyrus.

SERVE – Working for another person. Slaves worked without pay. Servants were paid. Slaves had to work for someone. Servants chose to do it. When we serve God, we should work for Him cheerfully.

SLAVERY – Keeping slaves was slavery. Slaves worked for a master. The master owned them. The master took care of his slaves, often poorly. He did not pay them wages. Some masters were cruel to their slaves.

SYNAGOGUE – The building where Jewish people worship and learn. Jesus went to the synagogue often to worship or teach.

TEMPT – To make us want to do something we should not do. Someone who tries to get us to do such things tempts us. Satan, the devil, tempted Jesus. He tried to get Jesus to do things He should not do. But Jesus would not do those things.

TEN COMMANDMENTS – God gave many rules, or laws, to Moses on Mount Sinai. They were given to help God's people know what to do and what not to do. Ten of those rules were special. God wrote them with His own hand on stone. The people then carried those two stones in a golden chest called the Ark of the Covenant. That chest was usually in the tabernacle or the temple.

VOW – Bible time people often made a vow to God. They promised to do certain things. People today make vows, too.